Lockdown

Lockdown

Diane Tullson

orca soundings

ORCA BOOK PUBLISHERS

Library and Archives Canada Cataloguing in Publication

Tullson, Diane, 1958-

Lockdown / written by Diane Tullson.
(Orca soundings)

ISBN 978-1-55143-918-1 (bound).--ISBN 978-1-55143-916-7 (pbk.)

I. Title. II. Series.
PS8589.U6055L62 2008   jC813'.6   C2007-906845-6

Summary: When a gunman is seen in the school, Adam and Zoe try
to make it out alive.

First published in the United States, 2008
Library of Congress Control Number: 2007940712

Orca Book Publishers gratefully acknowledges the support for its publishing
programs provided by the following agencies: the Government of Canada
through the Book Publishing Industry Development Program and the Canada
Council for the Arts, and the Province of British Columbia through the BC
Arts Council and the Book Publishing Tax Credit.

Cover design by Teresa Bubela
Cover photography by Getty Images

Orca Book Publishers
PO Box 5626 Station B
Victoria, BC Canada
V8R 6S4

Orca Book Publishers
PO Box 468
Custer, WA USA
98240-0468

www.orcabook.com
Printed and bound in Canada.
Printed on 100% PCW recycled paper.
12 11 10 09 • 5 4 3 2

For C.T. and R.T.

Acknowledgments

Thank you to the educators, all of you,
and to S.H. and K.D., always.

Chapter One

Science 10 is chaos. Josh's hamster had babies. It's Ms. Topett's classroom hamster, but Josh comes in at lunch to clean the cage. He takes the hamster home on weekends and holidays. It may as well be Josh's hamster. It's weird, the way Josh bonds with that hamster, but it's just one of many things that mark Josh as weird. For example, he always wears a blue shirt, the kind with buttons and a pocket. Always. He must have four or five blue shirts with buttons and a pocket.

No one wears blue shirts like that. Even if they wanted to, they wouldn't, because Josh always wears one. A blue shirt, jeans and boots—Josh always wears boots.

The hamster is an experiment. The hamster's coat is an unusual rusty red color—a genetic variation, Ms. Topett calls it. She bred the hamster with a normal amber-colored hamster to see if the young would have the darker color. We haven't seen the babies yet. Ms. Topett says it's too soon to disturb the nest. Right now, Ms. Topett is out of the classroom photocopying handouts. Before she left the room, Ms. Topett gave us direct orders to stay in our seats. But no one listened. Now, packed around the hamster cage, Science 10 wants to see the baby hamsters.

Josh stands with his hands jammed in his pockets, shifting his weight from one foot to the other. Josh outweighs me and I'm no lightweight. The idiots of Science 10 like to oink when Josh walks past. Hilarious. With one large index finger, Josh shoves his glasses back up onto his nose. He says, "We have to be quiet."

A girl, Natalie, pushes me to get to the table with the hamster cage. I let her past. Everyone lets her past—Natalie has that kind of power. She whines, "I can't see the babies."

I can't either. The mother hamster has them hidden in a cotton-ball nest. Natalie raps the metal cage with her fingernail. To Josh she says, "Make them come out."

Josh shakes his head. "The m-mother needs quiet. It's her first l-litter."

I watch Josh's face. When he stutters, it means he's stressed. When Josh gets stressed, he gets quiet. It reminds me of a storm, all the energy swirling in on itself. Once in a while Josh loses it, but it's amazing what he puts up with. The idiots of Science 10 have made this term a living hell for Josh.

Some of what they do is funny. I admit it, I've had a good laugh in this class. Like the time they told Josh, before class, that Ms. Topett was giving bonus marks that day for volunteers. So when Ms. Topett asked for volunteers, Josh stabbed his hand in the air to be picked. And he was. Josh ended up rolling a condom on a banana. His face went so red even his eyes filled with blood. Later, I could make him laugh about it too.

Now Natalie directs her gaze to the king of the idiots of Science 10: Chase. Chase is all talk, all the time. If there's one good thing about the way he targets Josh, it's that he leaves me alone. Chase slithers in front of Josh. He only comes up to Josh's chin, but Josh steps back. Chase says, "Who made you the freaking hamster expert? We just want to see them." He leans down to look right into the cage and slaps his hand on the desk. "Come on, mama. Come on out."

Josh has bright red spots on his cheeks. "You're scaring her."

Chase tilts the cage and lets it drop down on the desk. To Josh he says, "You're scaring it with your buggy eyes. I just want them to come out of the nest."

Josh blinks. I see him take a deep breath. Then he says, "They can't come out. They don't have their eyes open yet."

Natalie squeals, "Their eyes are still shut? I want to see!" She fumbles with the door in the top of the cage.

"No!" Josh swats her hand from the cage.

"Ow!" Natalie holds her hands up to her chin. She says to Chase, "He hit me, the loser."

I glance toward the door. Where is Ms. Topett?

Chase pushes Josh aside. To Natalie he says, "Don't bother reaching through the door. Just take the top off the cage." Chase releases the latches holding the cage to the tray and yanks off the cage top. Bits of cedar chips fly out onto the desk.

Josh gapes. The nest lies exposed in front of us. It is a mass of white cotton balls spun into one fluff pile. Bits of cedar and chewed toilet-paper roll weave among the cotton. It amazes me how the hamster can build this house, snug, warm, quiet.

Now, not so much. Chase pries the top from the cotton-ball nest. Natalie shoves in front of Chase and squeaks, "There they are!"

From where I'm standing, I can just see Josh's hamster coiled around four or five hairless pink babies. The mother hamster looks up at us with brown bead eyes. It scrambles to its feet. The babies wriggle in the sudden absence of their mother.

Natalie wrinkles her nose. "They're all naked."

Chase prods one of the babies with his finger. The mother hamster lunges at him. "Whoa!" Chase yanks his hand back. "She's vicious." He holds up his finger as if he's amazed he still has it. "She would have bitten it right off!"

Josh folds his arms over the tray. "W-we're scaring her. W-we have to leave her alone."

Ms. Topett enters the classroom. In a thundering voice, she commands, "Students, take your seats."

Most people return to their desks. Josh sets the cotton nest back over the babies and replaces the cage top. Ms. Topett levels her glare at Josh. "That means you too, Josh."

Josh doesn't seem to hear the teacher. He's staring at the cage. His eyes get wide.

Another student gets up and peers into the cage. He says, "Ew! She's eating one."

That's it. Everyone crowds around the

cage. Josh puts his hands on his face and shakes his head. "No. L-leave her alone. She's just m-moving them."

The mother hamster has carried one of the babies into a corner of the cage.

Ms. Topett pushes through the crowd of students. "If the mother feels threatened, she may try to move the nest." Ms. Topett scans our faces. Chase looks down. Natalie bats her eyes as if she doesn't know anything.

The mother hamster burrows into the nest and pulls out another of her young. She holds the baby in her mouth, her cheeks stretching around the wriggling pink mass. I wait for her to drop the baby with the other one.

One time last week, Josh fed his hamster peanuts one by one, and she packed them into her cheeks. She crammed ten peanuts in her cheeks.

Now she holds the baby the same way, her cheeks stretched so big that her eyes are slits. Then her eyes close and she tosses back her head.

Ms. Topett groans. "Oh no."

There is a collective gasp from the class-room.

Ms. Topett's voice is shrill. "Back to your seats. Everyone. NOW!"

We ignore her. The mother hamster takes the baby from the corner of the cage.

Josh starts to cry.

Half the class stands in stunned silence. The other half makes gagging noises.

The mother hamster heads into the nest. Ms. Topett grabs a jacket from the back of someone's chair and covers the cage. It's one of the idiots' jackets, apparently. He says, "Hey, you'll get it dirty!" and makes a move to retrieve the jacket.

Ms. Topett clamps her hand over his wrist. "Leave it."

With a scowl, he slumps into his seat.

Josh's face streams with tears. He's sobbing without making a sound, his huge chest heaving.

Ms. Topett turns to the class. Her voice shakes. "Sometimes this happens in nature. Sometimes, if conditions are harsh, like there isn't enough food."

Josh looks up in disbelief. He stops crying.

Ms. Topett continues, "Or if the mother feels the litter isn't strong enough to survive…"

Josh interrupts. "The mother had enough food. The babies were strong." He jabs his hand at the class. "They scared her. They wouldn't leave her alone."

Chase rolls his eyes. "This is a science class. The hamster is an experiment. Why did you have it in here if we weren't supposed to look?" He crosses his arms and leans back in his desk. "So we scared it. Big deal. We didn't mean to kill the babies."

Josh goes totally still. He looks from one student to the next. When he gets to me, I have to look away. There's something different about Josh, and it's like I don't recognize him anymore. He looks at each and every one of us. Then, without a word, he leaves the classroom.

After Josh leaves, Chase makes a mocking sound. "Oooh. I'm so scared."

People laugh.

Ms. Topett goes to the front of the classroom and, with a sigh, distributes her handouts. When the stack comes to me, I take one and hand the rest over my shoulder.

Then it occurs to me what was different about Josh. It wasn't that he looked different.

It was that he didn't stutter.

Chapter Two

At class change, I'm heading to the back door of the school when I feel Zoe slip up beside me. Gorgeous green-eyed Zoe. She smiles at me and threads her arm through mine. "Looks like you're making a break for it, Adam."

I nod. Second block is gym. Mr. Ellington makes us run when he doesn't feel like teaching, which is often. No pain, no gain, he always says. And he swears under his breath but you know what he's saying, and that's why everyone calls him Mr. Effington, even the jocks—but not to his face. I say to Zoe, "I'm going to grab a coffee. You can come along if you want."

Zoe looks at me for a second and then shakes her head. "No. I don't want to miss art class. We're working with clay. I love ceramic art. I love that it is what it is."

"Like a bowl," I say. "Or an urn."

She says, "Or you." Zoe breaks into a huge grin.

I probably like Zoe more than she likes me, but she's good at being a friend. She looks so happy, and the thing is, Zoe *is* happy. She could be heading into math or history, and she'd be happy. I say to her, "I'm happy for you that art class holds such appeal. For me, gym class holds only pain."

Zoe slings her pack over her shoulder. "Meet me back here for lunch, then."

"Caf is serving shepherd's pie today." I shudder. "Today is a really good day not to eat at school."

Zoe shrugs. "I brought a lunch. I'll share it with you."

And the thing is with happy people,

they expect you to be happy too. I smile. "Okay."

I imagine Zoe and I could be a couple if I ever gathered the nerve to take our friendship up a notch. Of course, I could be imagining that Zoe likes me. For me, it's easier to keep things the way they are. Less risky. Less to lose.

Zoe says, "Since you're here now, and you're meeting me for lunch, you may as well stay and go to second block."

I say, "That sounds like something Mr. Connor would say."

Mr. Connor is the principal. I've seen a fair bit of him lately. Apparently my attendance is a concern. More like my lack of attendance. Sometimes I cut gym and don't come back the rest of the day. Some days it's just easier not to go to school at all. I figure so long as I'm passing my courses, no one needs to get in a knot. Mr. Connor doesn't share my theory. Neither does Zoe, apparently. She says, "I like Mr. Connor. He brought his baby in to show us. He's not afraid to reveal he's human."

"Mr. Connor is human?"

She rolls her eyes.

I say, "I just need to get out of the school for a while. Science this morning was brutal." I tell Zoe about Josh and the hamster.

Zoe gasps. "Josh is your friend from Cook Training last term?"

Josh and I were in the same class. No one would work with him, so I did. I'm not sure that makes us friends. I say, "Josh and I shared a workstation, yes."

Zoe shakes her head. "He must be upset. Did anyone check if he was okay?"

I didn't. I was happy to get out of there. I say, "Yeah, he's fine."

Just then we see Josh in the hallway. He's carrying the hamster cage and heading for the door. He's walking fast, his eyes down, his shoulders hunched around his ears.

Zoe sighs. "Poor guy."

I could go talk to him, I guess. But the second bell rings and Zoe plants a quick kiss on my cheek. She says, "Meet me at my locker." I touch my cheek where she kissed me. I imagine what it would be like to kiss her. By the time I look back at Josh, he's already gone.

Chapter Three

Gym is right before lunch. If I were smart, I'd wait until the lunch bell rings to reappear at school. That way I could blend in with the crowds in the halls. Today, though, I make the mistake of arriving at school before the lunch bell rings. And Mr. Connor is waiting.

"Adam."

Mr. Connor must watch the back parking lot from a secret turret or something. How else would he know to wait for me at the back door? He's leaning against the wall, a half-eaten sandwich in his hand.

Mr. Connor is younger than a lot of teachers at this school. He wears khakis and running shoes. He's not wearing a necktie, but he'll have one slung over his desk chair. I know this from prior visits to Mr. Connor's office. He studies my eyes and repeats, "Adam." He says it like a challenge, like he doesn't want to believe he's caught me cutting class. Again. He extends his hand, ushering me into the school. "Glad you could make it."

I have to try. What have I got to lose? I say, "I pulled a hamstring. I have a note."

Mr. Connor tilts his chin. He takes a bite of his sandwich and watches me as he chews. He's waiting for me to say something even more stupid. I know from prior visits, Mr. Connor can wait a long time.

Sigh. I say, "I went for coffee."

Mr. Connor chews and swallows, takes another bite. The sandwich is just crust now, and shreds of lettuce. He takes the last bite and wipes his hand on his pants. He says,

"Did Mr. Ellington have you guys running in gym today?"

I follow him into the hall. I answer, "Apparently."

The halls are almost empty. Some classroom doors stand open, and as we pass I hear snips of lectures, but nothing makes sense. We pass the computer lab. Through the windows I see a pack of ninth-grade guys huddled over something they shouldn't be doing. One of the computer lab windows is already covered with its metal roll-down shutter. The lab will be closed at lunch. All the windows in the school have metal roll-down shutters, but only the computer lab closes the shutters. Except during drills. Then everything gets closed.

"Mr. Ellington used to make us run too."

I look at him in disbelief. "You had Mr. Ellington?"

Mr. Connor nods. "In this very school."

That explains how Mr. Connor always knows where to find me. I wonder what he called Mr. Ellington.

Mr. Connor stoops to pick up a balled-up piece of paper. He lobs it into a trash can. "In high school, I hated running track. It felt like running around in circles, which it is, I guess."

"I just don't like running."

"You might like it if you ran somewhere interesting."

I doubt it. I say, "You might be right."

Mr. Connor looks at me. "My son, Dylan, he likes running the seawall."

Mr. Connor has a picture of his family on his desk. His wife used to teach at this school too. Last time I saw Mrs. Connor, she was very pregnant. "Isn't your son just a baby?"

Mr. Connor grins. "I have a running stroller. Dylan rides, I run. He's helping me train for the half marathon next month."

"Half marathon." I shake my head.

"One step, that's how you start. Then another. No one sets out to run thirteen miles."

Mr. Connor isn't talking about running anymore.

We pass the cafeteria and the smell of shepherd's pie makes my stomach lurch. Cook

Training class last term cured me of eating caf food. A few students are already in the line-up. Half the school will cram into the caf at lunch.

Mr. Connor says, "Adam, you can run or not. It doesn't really matter to me. But cutting class isn't working for you, so it wouldn't hurt to do something else. You've got nothing to lose."

I smile. I was just thinking the same thing.

Mr. Connor's phone rings and he pulls it out of his pocket as he walks. It rings again and he flips it open. "Connor here."

He freezes, listening on the phone. His eyes narrow, then widen, like he can't believe what he's hearing. He lowers the phone. "Adam, you'll have to excuse me." He spins and walks away.

"No problem, Mr. Connor. Take all the time you need."

As he rounds the turn in the corridor, I see him break into a run.

Time for me to meet Zoe. All the time in the world. I smile to myself. How lucky is that?

Chapter Four

I climb the stairs to the second floor just as the lunch bell rings. Classroom doors burst open and students pour into the hallway. The hallway fills as people rush off to the cafeteria or gather in knots by their lockers to eat their lunch. A guy pushes past me, and my pack catches him in the shoulder. He puts his hand on my chest and pushes back, just hard enough that I know he's pissed, but not so hard that it counts as fighting. I see Zoe at her locker and plow through the throngs to reach her.

Zoe has silky hair she always wears in a ponytail. She calls it red but I think it's the color of new pennies. Zoe circles one arm around my neck and gives me a hug. She smells like peppermint lip balm and pottery clay from her art class. Into her ear I say, "Mr. Connor says I need some exercise. He says I should go for a walk on the seawall. He practically told me to cut classes this afternoon."

Zoe laughs. "If you're asking me to go with you, I'm tempted. But I have a math exam this afternoon and I have to study." She grabs her math text from the shelf in her locker. "You can help." She sits on the floor and tugs my hand to sit beside her.

I actually attend math class with some regularity. I like subjects that have right or wrong answers. Ambiguity bothers me. So does getting up in the morning. Sometimes it's just easier to stay in bed.

Expanding equations is almost pleasant, sitting here with Zoe. I watch as she works. She holds her pencil so that the knuckle on her first finger points up like a little mountain.

In the creases of her finger, I see traces of red clay.

Zoe looks up to find me gazing at her. She smiles in a way that makes me think if I had the nerve, I could kiss her right now.

I say, "Math is just like clay. It is what it is."

I imagine peppermint lip balm.

Zoe says, "Math is like poetry. The answer is hidden under layers and layers of symbols."

I imagine the kiss. Would she close her eyes?

I say, "All answers are hidden. Otherwise, everything is a given." I lean toward her.

She says, "Like feelings." She closes her eyes.

Then the alarm bell starts to clang.

Zoe's eyes fly open and she says, "Not another lockdown drill."

For a second the hall gets quiet. Then a collective groan lifts from the students in the hallway. Just last week we had a lockdown drill and now the same alarm is sounding. A few students glance around but no one seems too concerned.

Several girls standing at their lockers settle onto the floor and open their lunches. Another group laughs and jokes.

A teacher comes out of his classroom and shouts, "Lockdown, now!" When no one moves, the teacher takes the kid closest to him and shoves him into an open classroom. Then he strides over to the girls sitting on the floor and hauls one of them to her feet. She protests as he pushes her into the classroom. A few kids make their way into an open classroom. No one is moving fast.

I hoist myself to my feet. "Looks like your math exam got cancelled. How would you rather spend the afternoon—in a lockdown drill or avoiding school with me?"

Zoe rolls her eyes, but she lets me pull her to standing.

The teacher is herding kids into a classroom. He pulls one last student into the room and shouts, "Lock this door. No one goes in or out."

It's just a drill and this teacher is in full lockdown mode, totally whacked out on the thrill of the threat. I tug on Zoe's hand. "We'll take the back stairs."

The stairwell is empty, and we laugh as we take the stairs two at a time. We're still laughing when we reach the bottom of the stairs. Two things happen at the exact same time. First, we see the stairwell doors chained and padlocked. Then we hear Mr. Connor's voice over the PA. He says, "This is not a drill. There is a gunman in the school." The thin edge of fear in Mr. Connor's voice is totally real.

Chapter Five

It's like the entire school floods into the stairwell. People pound down the stairs toward us. Their voices clamor, frightened voices. They push and shove toward the blocked exit door, trying to escape the school.

Like fish in a bucket, that's what we are. My mouth goes dry. A locked stairwell seems like a good place to kill a lot of people at one time. I grab Zoe's hand. "Come on. We have to go back up."

We push against the flow of people, trying to get back up the stairs. As we run we scream, "The door is locked. It's a trap." When more people reach the locked door, they too push back up. Eventually, the tide of people tramples up the stairs and I have to hang on tight to Zoe.

At the second-floor landing, we find the doorway to the corridor jammed with people six or seven deep trying to get through to the classrooms. So many people are pushing at once that no one is moving. A big guy throws himself over the wall of people. I see his feet kicking against people's heads. He makes it over. More guys follow him. I feel someone climbing onto my back. Then a skate shoe slams against my cheek as the guy propels himself over the crowd. Girls are doing it too, clawing their way over the backs of their classmates, pulling on people's hair, digging their heels into people to get into the hallway.

I make a stirrup with my hands and shout at Zoe, "Give me your foot. I'll lift you up."

Zoe shakes her head. "I'm not leaving you." Just then the jam gives way and we pour into the hallway. It's all I can do to keep my footing. People run headlong, forcing others out of their way, piling into the classrooms. In front of me, a girl falls. Some people step around her. Most trample right over her. For a second I think about stepping over the girl too, but I bend down and pull her to her feet.

It's Natalie from Science 10. Her eyes are wild. She's crying, and mascara streams down her face. Her hair is tangled. Her shirt is ripped. She stumbles again and I grab her. People rush past us like we're not there. Guys are crying. People are screaming over and over, as if it is a ride. But it's not a ride. This is real.

I push Zoe and Natalie toward an open classroom door. The doorway is jammed with people trying to get in. I can see there must be fifty kids in the classroom. Some of the kids are under the desks. I wonder how they think that is going to help them escape from a shooter. Other students have rolled the shutters down over the windows. Someone shouts that people should get away from the walls. Would bullets go through a wall? Through a solid wood door? I doubt it. One thing I know: it's better to be in the classroom than in the open hallway. People are shouting, "Close the door! Close the door!"

I push the people in front of us so they sprawl into the classroom. The guy just ahead of us makes it into the classroom. Then he lunges for the door. "Close it!" he screams. "Lock it down!"

I know the guy. We have classes together.

I shout at him, "Not yet. Let us in!"

He looks me straight in the eye and slams the door.

I hear the lock thumping into place.

For a second, I stand, stunned. In lockdown drills, once the door is closed, no one comes in. So long as the door is closed and locked, students inside will be safe. But students outside are screwed. That's how it works. And those bastards just shut the door on Zoe, me and Natalie.

All down the hall, doors slam closed. We're alone in the hallway. I hit the door with my shoulder.

Zoe's hair has slipped out of its ponytail. She's not crying, but her eyes are so wide, her skin so white, I think she could be disappearing.

I crash against the door. "Let us in!" I throw myself against the door and actually feel it shudder. Voices on the other side are angry, afraid I'll break the door.

Natalie wails, "You're leaving us out here to die!"

If they don't open the door for Natalie, they'll never open it for me. I hit the door again and again. Zoe puts her hands on my shoulders. I am so panicked I can barely feel her touch. She says, "Adam, we have to move."

Where? The classrooms are locked down and we're locked out. And it's my fault because I wanted to leave the school. Instead of getting in a classroom when we had the chance, I wasted our time trying to leave.

Zoe takes my hand. Suddenly, I can feel her touch again, feel that she's still here.

"Now, Adam."

We look down at Natalie. She's slipped to her knees, rocking, her hands over her ears. Zoe reaches for one of Natalie's hands and I grab the other. We yank her to her feet and start to run just as we hear the first shots.

Chapter Six

The shots sound at a distance, on the main floor, maybe at the office. Between Zoe and me, Natalie stumbles. I yank on her hand. "Get up!"

Zoe throws me a look. She speaks gently to Natalie. "We have to get out of the hall. Can you keep up with us?"

Natalie nods.

We take off down the hall. The classroom doors are closed, all of them. Behind the doors, I can hear people's frightened voices. Try being out in the hall, I think to myself.

At the boy's washroom, we push against the door and it opens. If we can get in, so can the shooter, but it's better than being in the open hallway. We jam into the washroom.

A guy I know, Baker, is sitting on the sink. As we burst in, his eyes get really wide and he drops a smoldering butt into the sink. Exhaling, he says, "You scared me, man. I thought you were Connor, going to bust me."

Natalie stops blubbering. Zoe blinks. Didn't he hear the alarm? I wave away the cloud of smoke and say, "Uh, Baker, you know there's a lockdown, right?"

With his eyes narrowed against the smoke, he looks at Zoe and Natalie. "What are you two doing in here? This is the boys' can, isn't it?" He looks around as if he isn't sure.

I say, "Baker, it's a real lockdown. It's not a drill."

Baker's eyebrows lift. He reaches into the sink to retrieve his smoke.

"Baker, there's a shooter in the school."

As if on cue, we hear the sound of gunshots, closer than before.

Baker swears under his breath. He launches himself off the sink and into the toilet cubicle.

Zoe pulls Natalie farther away from the door. There's no lock on the washroom door, no surprise. One cubicle. Three urinals. A partition between the door and the urinals.

More gunshots, and now there is no denying it—the shots are very close.

I push Zoe and Natalie into the cubicle. "Get up on the toilet. If the shooter just looks under the door, maybe he'll think no one is in here."

It's lame and we all know it. Natalie starts to cry again.

I say, "Of course, if he hears us, he'll blast us all."

Natalie shuts up.

Baker crouches with his feet on the toilet seat. He must have size thirteen feet, and there is no way we're all going to fit up there with him, not unless one of us stands in the toilet, which I'm prepared to do right about now.

More gunfire and it's close. Even in the washroom, I can hear screaming voices from the classrooms. The shooter can't get into the classrooms, not with the lockdown. I guess he could blow a classroom door lock, but from the way he's moved through the school, it appears more random. He doesn't seem to be spending much time in any one place.

Natalie and Zoe fold themselves around Baker on the toilet seat. Natalie pulls out her phone.

Everyone with a cell phone must have phoned 911 by now. Where the hell are the cops?

Zoe says, "Natalie, you're not actually calling someone, are you?"

Natalie gives Zoe a "yeah, duh" look.

Zoe says, "Because you can't make a sound."

Natalie says, "Oh. Right." And she closes the phone.

More shots and they're so close that I don't stop to think about it. I jump up onto the toilet seat. If I face the door of the cubicle and perch with only my heels on the seat, I can just fit.

The gunshots stop. I want to reach for Zoe, I want to hear her voice. As if Baker can read my mind, he whispers, "Easy, man."

For a long time it's quiet. Then I hear two things. First, the classroom noise filtering into the hallway gets louder. That means someone has opened the washroom door. I feel Baker tense. I'd like to scream except I can't even breathe. The second sound I hear is the chirpy ringtone of Natalie's cell phone.

Thank you, Natalie. We might as well hang a sign on the door, *Here we are*.

She silences the phone.

Sweat runs into my eyes but I don't dare move to wipe it away. Baker is weirdly still. The hallway sound recedes and I hear the washroom door close. Is he gone? Did he leave?

Footsteps. Heavy footsteps. He's here.

My knees go liquid and it's all I can do to keep my balance.

The footsteps pause outside the cubicle.

I hear him laugh, softly at first, then more loudly. Then the cubicle door opens.

He's wearing a blue shirt with buttons and a pocket. He's got a gun in his hand. Our eyes lock. He stops laughing.

The shooter is Josh.

The gun comes up.

Maybe I'll stop the bullets. Maybe Baker won't get hit. Maybe Josh will shoot me and leave the others.

I feel suddenly ice cold.

I watch Josh close his finger over the trigger.

Did I feed the dog this morning? I can't remember if I fed the dog.

I smell piss.

The sound of the gun rockets inside my head, and I clamp my eyes closed and scream. Everyone is screaming, even Josh, and then he shoots again and it's totally dark inside the washroom.

Chapter Seven

Somewhere it registers that I'm not dead, but it takes Baker stepping into the toilet bowl to convince me. Baker shakes off his foot, cursing. I feel drops of toilet water spray my face. Okay, I'm not dead.

I stumble off the toilet seat, my legs barely able to take my weight. "Zoe?" Broken glass crunches under my feet. "Zoe!"

"I'm fine." I feel her hands on my chest. "Are you hurt?"

"No." My voice is a croak.

I hear the snap of a lighter, and Baker's face appears in the small circle of flame. "He shot out the light," Baker says. He shovels the broken glass out of the way with his shoe.

In the pale pool of light, the four of us stand, stunned. When I look at Natalie, I gasp. Blood is running from under her hair. Baker must see it too. He says to her, "You better sit down."

Natalie touches her fingers against her chin. When she sees the blood, her eyes get big.

I grab Natalie and lower her to the floor. Zoe rips out a sheaf of paper towel and presses it to the side of Natalie's head.

Natalie starts to howl.

I'm no doctor, but based on her volume, she doesn't seem to be badly hurt. I say to Baker, "Hold the lighter up."

Baker says, "You want me to open the door, get the light from the hall?"

Zoe and I reply at once. "No!"

Baker shrugs. He holds the lighter close to Natalie's head. Zoe eases away the wad of paper towel. The blood seems to be oozing from just over Natalie's right ear. Gently, I run my hand over her scalp. Except for the blood, her skull feels like it should. I say to her, "A bullet must have grazed your head."

Grazed her head. As in, barely missed shattering her skull. As in, barely missed splattering her brain. I replace Zoe's hand against the wound, pressing her hand for a moment.

Baker whips off his shirt and wraps it around Natalie. "Gotta keep her warm." He gathers Natalie against his chest. "Here. Lean back. I've got you."

Baker must be the most unlikely Boy Scout, but Natalie settles against him. Her howling subsides to hiccupping sobs. It's clear now that the smell of pee was Natalie's. If Baker notices, he ignores it. Natalie opens her cell phone and starts punching the keys.

"The bleeding seems to have stopped." Zoe peers under the paper towel. She grabs a clean stack and hands them to Baker. He holds them to Natalie's head. Zoe straightens up.

I pull her into a hug and burrow my nose

in her hair. "Are you crying?" I hold her so that I can see her face. "You are." I offer her my sleeve to wipe her face. "He won't be back, Zoe. If he meant to kill us, he would have."

"He got Natalie."

"I think a bullet ricocheted and got Natalie."

"He still got her. He could have killed her."

"But he didn't."

Baker looks up at us. "Weird. I wonder why he didn't kill us."

I think of the way Josh looked when he found us in the stall. Gleeful. I shudder thinking about it. Then he recognized me. He was surprised at first, and then, I don't know, the look in his eyes changed. He was disappointed maybe. Maybe pissed. Pissed that the kid he finds is the one kid in the entire school he might have been able to call a friend.

I say, "His name is Josh. He won't be back here, but I don't think he's done."

Chapter Eight

I feel everyone looking at me. I'm sweating again. Big fat pellets of sweat run down my face. Zoe breaks free of my hug. "It was Josh? Josh with the hamster?"

Natalie gets very quiet.

Baker says, "Who is Josh?"

Baker is in my grade along with Josh. I say, "You know Josh. Glasses. Kind of big. Always wears a blue shirt."

Baker casts his eyes up and furrows his brow. Finally, he says, "Nope. I've never seen him before."

Baker must attend class even less than I do. I say, "Anyway, it's Josh. He's just a guy."

Zoe plants her hands on her hips. "Just a guy with a gun."

Baker nods. "My uncle has a gun just like he had. Snub-nosed revolver. My uncle hides it in the garage."

Not much of a hiding place if Baker knows where to find it.

Baker continues, "My uncle was supposed to turn it in, but he said he forgot. He uses a half-moon clip dealie, loads six rounds at a time."

Zoe says, "Nice. He can kill six people without reloading."

Baker shrugs. "It's a small gun. It's not exactly an assault weapon."

Zoe turns to me. "How long has Josh been planning this?"

"You're talking as if I knew something about this. I didn't know he was going to shoot up the school."

But I remember how Josh looked at us in science, how he seemed to record our faces. My mouth goes dry.

Maybe Natalie is thinking the same thing. She says, "Chase is an ass. He went too far with the hamster."

Chase is an ass, but I'm surprised to hear Natalie say so. Natalie and Chase are in the alliance of Science 10 idiots. Natalie seems to have forgotten her role in the hamster-eating drama. I say, "It's not like anyone stepped in to stop Chase."

Natalie detects the barb in my statement. "So this is my fault? No way," she says. "Josh is crazy, everyone knows that. He was crazy before the hamster thing."

I say, "I didn't mean it's your fault. I mean, no one stepped in. So maybe it's everyone's fault. And anyway, Josh isn't crazy. He's just different."

Baker nods. "Totally. Normal to the extreme."

Zoe looks at him in disbelief. "You're saying Josh is normal?"

Baker says, "It's not like I'd ever do it, but you've never thought about offing someone?"

Zoe says, "No!"

Natalie shrugs. "Whatever."

I say, "We could try to stop him."

Zoe snorts. "How?"

Zoe's right, I know she is. What are we going to do against a guy with a gun? All the time you hear about shooters and you think, How could he shoot so many people? Why didn't someone just take him down?

Zoe says, "We can't go out there, Adam. We'll get shot. We were lucky once but we won't be lucky again. We'll get caught and we'll get killed."

I look at her. She looks different, but I guess no one looks normal when they're scared. I say to her, "If we don't stop Josh, he'll either get shot by the police or he'll shoot himself."

"So?" Zoe retorts. "Let's hope he blows his brains out before he finds someone else to shoot."

Zoe's mad, and who could blame her? Nothing makes it right, what Josh is doing. But I think about all those times I've seen people push him around. There must be a hundred more incidents I don't know about.

Maybe Josh has lived his whole life being pushed around.

I say, "You don't know Josh."

"I don't need to know him."

"He's not like us."

"No? Really? Like, we don't take a gun to school to settle our differences?"

Baker and Natalie watch the exchange as if they're watching a tennis match.

I say, "He didn't shoot me. He didn't shoot us. Maybe I can talk to him. Maybe I can stop this whole thing."

Zoe is quiet for a long moment. Then she says, "Whose side are you on?"

I swallow. "It's not about sides."

She says, "Of course it's about sides. What else is this about? Either you're on his side or you're on our side."

Our side. Not her side. I reach out my hands but she bats them away. She says, "Think about this, Adam. The guy has a gun and he's probably killed people. He's out there now trying to kill more people."

As if to punctuate her statement, we hear distant shots.

"There." Her mouth tightens. "Maybe he's found someone else cowering in a can. Or maybe he's pinned them against the chained exit door. Maybe he's picking them off one by one."

The sound of the shots makes my stomach flip. "Zoe, I have to try."

Zoe jabs me in the chest. "I know he's friggin' crazy, and if you go out there after him, then you're crazy too. If you go out there, you're an idiot and a loser, just like him."

I blink. It feels like the floor has shifted under my feet. Like the earth has tilted a different direction. I search Zoe's eyes for a sign of what we had, but all I see is fear and anger. Eyes that just an hour ago held warmth now chill me. Her words yank my guts like she's turning me inside out. When I can speak, I say to her, "So you have nothing to lose."

Baker clears his throat. When he speaks, his voice is quiet. "If I wanted to shoot up the school, I'd hit the caf. That's where I'd find the most people."

Baker and I exchange a look. He's right.

Zoe says, "The cafeteria is locked down. He won't get in."

I think about Cook Training class last term, how Josh and I used to goof off in the supply hall behind the kitchen. It connects to the theater concession and, from there, the theater. During school performances, the concession sells coffee and snacks. Between performances, like now, the concession is just an unlocked storage area for stage props. One time last term, Josh and I used the supply hall to find our way into the darkened theater, and we sat there for the entire cooking class. Being there was as good as vanishing from the school.

I say, "Josh could get into the caf." I tell them about the little-used corridor from the theater to the kitchen. "He doesn't even have to use the locked stairwells. He can enter the theater up here through the second-floor doors. If anyone was in the theater when the alarm sounded, they'll be locked-down backstage."

Baker nods. "So even if the cops are in the main halls, Josh can get into the caf."

"But the last shots we heard were in the other direction," Zoe says. "They sounded like he was heading away from the theater."

Baker shrugs. "The school will be crawling with cops. If this Josh guy is going to move anywhere without getting spotted, he'll have to use that back hallway. He'll double back."

Natalie offers me her phone. "Tell the cops. They'll find him."

I wave away the phone. "You call them. But they'll be too late." I head to the door.

Zoe looks like she's going to cry again. "You could be too late, Adam."

I struggle to find enough spit to speak. "Then I have nothing to lose either."

Chapter Nine

As soon as I'm outside the washroom, I regret my decision. Every instinct is to hide from Josh, to run as fast as possible in the other direction. It's exactly the feeling I get when I watch scary movies, like my bones have gone to mush. But this feeling is more. Way more. I'm so scared that I have to tell my feet to move.

The hallway is empty. People's lunches are scattered around from before the lock-down. Locker doors swing open. Being in this hallway is like being in a dead place. I stay as close as I can to the wall—not that the wall gives me any cover. It's just that, close to the wall, I know there's one side he can't get me from.

The second-floor theater door is down a smaller hallway off the main corridor. At the corner, I pause. I can't see around the corner, of course, and I don't want to walk straight into Josh. I feel ridiculous doing it, but I extend my arm around the corner and wave my hand. If Josh is taking aim, maybe he'll shoot my hand before he shoots me in the head. I peer around the corner. No Josh. The hall is empty. With a jagged breath of relief, I make the turn.

At the theater door, I listen. I can't hear anything from behind the door. If the door is locked, I'll have no choice but to go back to Zoe and the others.

Please don't open. Please don't open.

I try the handle. It opens.

I step inside the theater and let the door close behind me. The theater is dark, lit only by the exit markers. The vast silence of the space greets me with the coolness of a cave. I'm aware of the sound of my breath, panting, as if I'd been running. I blink, trying to get used to the murky darkness of the theater. Finally, I can make out the rows of seats and the stage area, below.

I remember this from when Josh and I sat in here. If you sit still and don't make a sound, it's dark enough that someone could look in and not see you. It's like the way a rabbit stays still, and its brown fur makes it disappear in the grass. The rabbit is there, but unless you know it's there, you'll never see it. So it's like it's not there.

If Josh is sitting quietly in the theater, he could be watching me right now and I wouldn't know it. New sweat squirts under my arms. I scan the rows. If he's crouched down between the seats, I'd never see him. Not until he jumped up and aimed his gun at my head. My feet freeze. I'm the rabbit. Josh is the hunter.

This morning, he was just Josh. Last night, when he brushed his teeth and said goodnight to his parents, he was just Josh. I met his parents last term, when the cooking class hosted the parents to a dinner. My parents came in the clothes they wore to work. Josh's parents looked like they were going to church. Josh's dad wore a suit with one of those poofy pocket handkerchiefs. His mom wore a string of pearls at her neck. They were so proud of Josh, so happy to sit at a table and have him serve them food that he'd made himself.

When did it happen? When did he go from being just Josh to who he is now? Maybe he's been thinking about this for a long time. Maybe last term, when he and I sat in this theater, he was thinking about it.

Josh isn't here. I have to tell myself that or I can't make my feet move. He's not here. I take another step down. He's not here. I step down from one row of seats to the other, then another. If Josh were here, I'd already be dead. But maybe he's waiting until he has an easy shot. Fear freezes my feet to the step.

When Josh found us in the washroom, when he was aiming that gun at us in the stall, I didn't feel fear, not like this. In the washroom, it was like I resigned myself to being dead. But now, as I stalk him through the school, I'm making a choice to face him and that gun again, and it scares the crap out of me. I bolt down the steps all the way to the bottom.

He's not here. I feel almost giddy as I reach the concession door. He's not here. My chest is heaving. He's not here.

But that means he could be anywhere.

At the concession door, I stop again. I know Josh isn't in the theater. I could just hide in the theater. I could hide between the rows and no one would see me. I could wait here until the cops storm the school. No one would blame me. Anyone in his right mind is holed up somewhere, finding religion. I don't have to stop Josh. It's not like I'm Josh's friend. I barely know the guy. I'm just in some classes with him.

I think about the guy who locked Zoe, Natalie and me out of the classroom. His name is Justin or Jordan or something. I know him too.

Earlier today, in science, if I'd said

something, would it have made a difference? I could have tried to stop Chase from opening the hamster cage. I could have stepped between Chase and the cage, told Chase what a weenie he is for tormenting Josh. But I didn't. Josh probably thinks I'm just as bad as Chase.

I can hide, or I can face Josh. I gaze around the darkened theater. A few moments ago I was scared to be here, but now the theater feels like a refuge.

I have to try. I yank open the concession door and step in.

Chapter Ten

The door closes behind me. If it was dark in the theater, the concession is pitch-black. I fumble for a light switch. The walls feel cool, and I feel a hundred scrapes and divots, but I can't feel a switch. I know the concession has two doors: one to the theater and one to the cafeteria supply hall. I can just make out the door to the supply hall from the crack of light that appears under that door.

I've heard that people who can't see develop a keen sense of hearing and touch so that they "see" their world through the other senses. In the dark, every one of my nerve endings is tingling. I can smell dust. I can smell latex paint from stage backdrops. I can taste the darkness. I reach my hand out in front of me. Nothing. I sweep my hand through the air. Nothing. I take a step.

Immediately, my knee cracks into something hard and metal. I suck in a breath. Whatever I just walked into clatters to the floor. The noise makes me jump back against the door. I laugh because it's so stupid, what I'm imagining: that Josh is in here with me.

I stand still and wait for my heart to stop pounding. It takes a long time. I'm breathing so hard that I can't hear anything else, so I hold my breath and listen.

Now blood pulses in my temples, and I stifle the need to breathe because I can hear him. I can. Not in here. Out there. I can hear someone breathing on the other side of the door.

My throat closes. I want to cough. Don't cough. Don't make a sound. I wring enough spit to swallow.

It's too late to hide. Josh knows I'm in here. Maybe he's waiting for me to make another move. Maybe he's giving me a chance to get away, a chance to find somewhere to hide.

Between Josh and me is the supply hall. And beyond the supply hall, hundreds of people hide. Hundreds of people who think they're safe. Hundreds of people who thought this morning they were just going to school. Maybe they hugged their little sister. Probably not. Maybe they told their old man they loved him. Probably not.

I fed the dog this morning, I remember now. Our dog's name is Festus. He's a black lab cross we rescued from the pound. He drools when I feed him so I make him wait on his carpet, but this morning I forgot and I stepped in his drool with my bare feet. It was a cold slippery rope that slimed my foot. I wiped my foot on the leg of my jeans. When I dumped his food in his bowl, Festus thumped his tail against the cupboard like a drum. *Thump thump thump*. His dog tags clanked against the metal bowl as he ate, and I thought for the thousandth time, does that bother him, those tags making such a racket as he eats?

Tomorrow, someone will feed the dog. The day after that, they'll feed him again. And each time they feed him, the dog's tags will clank on the bowl, and the dog won't give a damn because that's the way it's always been. For Festus, it's normal. For Festus, it's just what it is.

Tomorrow, someone will feed the dog and it'll be a normal morning. Except their kid will be dead.

In a way, it would be easier if Josh put the gun against my head and blasted me away.

Slowly, carefully, I stretch my hands out in front of me. When I feel nothing, I take a step.

And I trip over whatever crashed a minute ago. I slam down onto my knees. The pain makes my eyes water. On my hands and knees, I fix my stare on the crack of light under the far door. I feel the floor ahead of me for a clear path. I set my hand in something wet. It's cold and sticky, and for a second I think of Festus and his drool.

Then it occurs to me. I've put my hand in blood.

I bolt to my feet and crash toward the door. I trip, get up, trip again. I feel my own blood soaking one knee of my jeans. In full-blown panic, I reach the door and am scrabbling for the handle when the overhead light comes on.

Chapter Eleven

Instinctively, I cover my head.

"Adam?"

It's Zoe. I blink in the sudden glare of the concession light. I look up to see Zoe at the theater door, her face drawn and pale.

She's the most beautiful sight.

She says, "It sounded like you were wrestling six people in here." Zoe picks her way over the heaps of backdrops that I've trashed and kneels down beside me. She says, "What are you doing, crashing around in the dark?"

I look at my hands, at the floor. No dead body. The sticky stuff seems to be from an oozing canister of Coke syrup. I wipe my hands on my pants. I say, "I couldn't find the light switch."

"It's on the outside, by the door." Zoe smiles. "You just have to know where to look."

I say, "You shouldn't be here, Zoe."

She touches my face. "I couldn't let you get yourself killed, Adam."

My relief is so huge that I almost laugh. I grab Zoe into a hug. She melts against me. I bury my face in the warm crook of her neck. Her hair is damp and she smells a bit like sweat. It's a nice smell, though, and I breathe it in. She says, "I'm sorry for the things I said. I'm just so scared."

I shake my head. "It's all right. I'm not scared at all."

She laughs.

I say, "I just want to turn back time. I want to go back to before this happened."

Zoe says, "I want to go back to when we were at my locker." She pulls away so she can see my face. "Before the lockdown, when we were at my locker, you were going to kiss me."

I feel my face turn red. Was it so obvious?

She says, "Do you know how long I've waited for that kiss?"

Yes, I think to myself, I know how long I've waited. Months. Since the first day of last term when I sat with her in Planning and thought she was the most beautiful girl I'd ever seen.

I smooth a strand of hair from her cheek. "I didn't want to risk it."

"Risk it." She closes her eyes.

I touch my finger to her lips. Soft. She smiles. Her teeth are perfectly white. I rest my hands on her hips and pull her closer. I can almost forget where we are. Almost. I say, "Zoe, this is crazy. Josh could storm in here any minute. You need to hide."

Zoe shrugs. "You can't do this alone. I'm not sure you can do it at all. But if you're willing to try, so am I."

She feels so good in my arms I almost

believe that we can do it. "You left Natalie with Baker?"

"He said he had something to calm them down. I didn't ask what."

Trust Baker.

Zoe continues, "Adam, when we're through this, I want to go for that walk on the seawall."

I hold her tight. "We will."

She says, "Josh and the hamster, it wasn't your fault. No one expects you to be a hero."

"That's the thing, Zoe. I'm not a hero. But I can't keep living with my head in the sand."

She says, "Why now?"

I look at her. "Why now what?"

She studies my face as if she's looking at me for the first time. "Why now, Adam? Why step up now, when there's everything at stake?"

I've seen Zoe carry spiders by their web and set them outside. With the spider, Josh would do the same thing. He can't squash a bug, but he's prepared to blow apart the school.

I can't tell Zoe about Josh. I'm not sure

it's clear, even to me, what motivates the guy. He's fed up with how people treat him, for sure. Chase is an ass. So are a hundred other guys. For me, Chase isn't the reason I cut school. I'm not sure why I cut school, except that if you cut once and then you cut again, it just gets easier not to come back. It's not like it feels good. It just starts to feel normal. Maybe it's the same with Chase. He started acting like an ass, and now it feels normal.

Maybe Baker is right. For Josh, normal has slid to the extreme.

I'm not ready to admit to Zoe that on some level I knew this was coming. I've always known. It could have been Josh. It could have been a hundred other guys—guys way more likely than Josh to be violent. Baker is right. On some level, I could do what Josh is doing.

Everyone loves Zoe. Zoe can walk into a room full of strangers and just expect that people will like her. I don't think Josh has ever felt like that.

I rest my cheek against Zoe's hair and answer. "Maybe I'm stepping up because now everything is at stake."

Chapter Twelve

The supply corridor between the theater concession and the cafeteria still has the original flooring from when the school was built. Once-white tiles alternate with a color somewhere between pumpkin and puke. Near the walls, both colors of tile are obscured by a gray buildup of filth so thick you could scratch your name in it. The walls are striped with black marks from generations of caf students and staff driving into the walls with loaded carts. Along the walls, carts are stacked with clean banquet dishes, pallets of canned goods and cafeteria supplies. The hallway smells of old grease.

We don't really have a plan, Zoe and I.

The corridor winds around several corners, tracing the contours of the theater on one side, the cafeteria on the other. Through the walls on the cafeteria side, Zoe and I can hear the hum of frightened voices.

Josh's plan, or what we think is his plan, is to use this hallway to enter the open kitchen. From there, he'd have full and easy access to the cafeteria. And all the students in it. The kitchen is at the end of the hallway we're in, behind a set of swinging metal doors.

The thing is, we don't know where Josh is. We haven't heard shots for a while. He could be behind us, maybe in the theater or concession. He could be ahead of us, waiting in the hallway. For now, the hum of voices from the cafeteria is soothing reassurance that he isn't in there. Yet.

Zoe takes my hand. I give it a squeeze. We inch down the hall, clinging to the walls. When we can, we dive between carts or pallets to wait and listen. Then we make another silent step, and another, to the next hiding place.

Closer to the caf, more carts are lined up along the hallway. We dodge between the carts, finding what cover we can. We watch ahead and behind us for Josh. I want to believe that he's not even here, but Baker is right: If Josh wants to shoot people, he'll find them in the caf. And Josh knows about this corridor. He's the one who showed it to me.

If Zoe and I wanted to change our minds, we couldn't, because it would mean retracing our steps, maybe right into Josh's path. We can only go forward, not knowing what we'll find around each bend in the hallway. My mouth is so dry that I've given up trying to swallow. The skin inside my throat feels like leather.

My hands, though, drip with nervous sweat. I'd like to wipe them on my pants, but that would mean letting go of Zoe's hand, and I'm not about to do that. It feels like I've been waiting all my life to have her hand in mine.

I think of Natalie and how close that bullet came to her head. I think of the blood, of how much more blood there might have been. I pull Zoe a little closer.

How bad is it out there? How many kids are sprawled in pools of their own blood?

The only thing I know for sure is that I couldn't stand it if Zoe were hit. If Zoe were hit, nothing would be worth anything.

Zoe and I slip in between a cart of banquet plates and a drum of cooking oil. With my mouth close to her ear, I whisper, "You stay here. I'll go ahead on my own."

Her eyebrows furrow and she shakes her head. No.

"Just until I know it's clear. Then I'll motion for you to come." I reach my hand out from our hiding place and wave it.

Zoe crosses her arms. She's not happy, but I'm prepared to ignore that.

I motion for her to crouch down low beside the oil drum. She's small enough that she can almost fit between the drum and the wall. You'd have to be looking for her to see her.

Please, don't look for her. Please.

I kiss her forehead, and she gives me a small smile.

I head out into the hallway. I have to zigzag across the hall to find cover between two pallets. From where I crouch, I can see the end of the hallway and the metal doors into the kitchen. I cross the hall again and jam myself between two pallets of mayonnaise. One of the enormous plastic containers of mayo is split along the seam, and the smell of spoiled mayo makes my stomach turn.

At first I think I imagine it. I take a breath and try to hear over the pounding of my heart in my ears. Then I make it out—the sound of someone talking.

Someone else is in the hallway.

I gesture wildly for Zoe to stay put. I can only hope she sees me.

I peer in the direction of the voice. I can't see anyone. The person is hiding too. I can't make out any words, just a voice speaking barely above a whisper. Gathering a breath, I move once more across the hall.

From my new hiding place, I hear that

the voice is a man's. I strain to hear what the person is saying. I hear bits of it, the words "supply corridor." It's like he's giving orders. It sounds like he's on the same side of the hall as me.

I wonder if I can look under this cart. I bend down and put my cheek against the floor. The floor feels gritty. I push my face hard against the floor to see under the cart. It's amazing what's under the cart, out of reach of any occasional broom. With my butt in the air, my face crammed against the floor, I can make out the guy's shoes.

Running shoes. I let out my breath—so it's not Josh!

The shoes are serious running shoes, for serious runners. I listen to the voice and it is suddenly familiar.

It's Mr. Connor! He must be talking on his cell phone. Trust Mr. Connor to know about this corridor. He must have figured out, like we did, that this is the most likely path for Josh. He's waiting for Josh.

I feel like bursting out of my hiding place. But something makes me move quietly, and

I creep across the hall into a recess between two carts, right across from Mr. Connor.

Mr. Connor is sitting on the floor, his knees drawn up, his head hanging over his knees, his hand over his forehead, rubbing his eyebrows. He doesn't see me. He's got a cell phone held up to one ear. He's doing most of the talking.

I hear the lightest of gasps coming from where I left Zoe.

Mr. Connor is intent on his conversation.

I strain to hear, to know what's happening with Zoe.

Then I hear. Footsteps. Heavy footsteps. The kind of footsteps boots make. Coming down the hall toward us.

Chapter Thirteen

Inside my head, I scream at Mr. Connor, "Shut up! Josh will hear you!"

Mr. Connor continues to talk into the phone.

I wave my hands in the air, trying to attract his attention. Still, he keeps his eyes glued to his lap. Mr. Connor is more agitated now, and his voice is louder. Josh would have to be deaf not to hear him.

Please, Zoe, do not move.

I imagine Zoe as a rabbit, blending in to the wall behind her.

The footsteps continue without pause past where Zoe is hiding.

Thank you. Thank you.

If Mr. Connor weren't so busy with the phone, maybe he'd hear the footsteps coming right for him. Why doesn't he shut up? I think about throwing a coin at him to get his attention, but the footsteps approach and I shrink back against the wall.

Don't move a muscle. Don't even breathe.

The footsteps stop. Only moving my eyes, I see the toe of one of Josh's boots. He takes another step and now I can see his entire profile.

Oh. My.

Josh is so close I could touch him. The gun is in his right hand, hanging straight down. I could reach out and grab the gun. Except that I can't move. Josh stands still. His shirt shows dark-blue wet circles under the arms. I see sweat running down the side of his face.

If Josh turned his head, he would look right at me. I mentally shrink myself. But

Josh doesn't look in my direction. He's looking across from me, at Mr. Connor. Josh seems intent on Mr. Connor's voice. He looks calm. Scary calm. His right hand squeezes the handle of the gun.

Josh takes another step. He's right between me and Mr. Connor. I can't see Mr. Connor anymore because Josh is between us. Josh turns to face Mr. Connor.

Mr. Connor stops talking. I hear the cell phone clatter to the floor.

Josh is looking right at him. He raises the gun.

I hear Mr. Connor say "Please."

Then Josh fires the gun.

Chapter Fourteen

The blast echoes in the hallway and I cover my ears. Josh steps back and wipes something from his cheek. His hand comes away red. I taste puke and swallow it.

I can hear Mr. Connor crying. At least he's not dead.

Josh looks back up the hall toward Zoe, and I pray that she hasn't made a sound. Does he know she's there? Is he going to finish Mr. Connor and then go for Zoe? Josh turns back to Mr. Connor and once again raises the gun.

There's no time for conscious thought. On liquid knees I launch myself from between the carts. Josh hears me and spins. But I hit him with my full weight and he crumples to the floor.

Josh snakes beneath me. I wrap my hand around his right wrist, amazed at his strength, appalled at my weakness. My hands are slippery with sweat. He swears at me. I feel his knee come up between my legs. My eyes go black and I gasp for breath. He's on top of me now. With everything I've got, I haul on his wrist, the gun just inches from my head. My hand slips, and his wrist pulls away.

Just before you die, your life flashes before your eyes. Not so. Just before you die, you piss yourself. Josh's finger squeezes against the trigger. But the gun isn't coming toward me. It's going to Josh's own head.

My right fist crashes against Josh's cheek. Blood from his nose sprays me in the face. His eyes squeeze shut against the pain, and he lowers the gun. I hit him again as I grab for the gun. I hit him once more and now I have the gun. I flip Josh onto the floor and point the gun at his head.

When I can suck in a breath, I scream, "Zoe, run!"

Josh looks up at me. It's like there's nothing left of him behind his eyes.

I sense Zoe standing in the hall. Again, I scream at her, "Run!"

But she won't run. She stands stock-still, staring down the hall.

I turn and look. Mr. Connor is on his feet, not a mark on him. Near where he was hiding, a burst can of ketchup drips from a pallet onto the floor. And behind Mr. Connor, at the metal swinging doors, about ten fully armed police officers aim guns at me.

Chapter Fifteen

"Drop your weapon! Down on the floor!"

The police are dressed head to toe in blue tactical suits. Their faces are covered with goggles and Kevlar face masks over their mouths. They're shouldering submachine guns. And they're screaming at me. I'm the one holding the gun. They think I'm the shooter.

I look down at Josh. If I drop the gun, he'll pick it up. He'll shoot me or he'll shoot Zoe. Or he'll shoot a cop. Best-case scenario, he'll shoot himself, but I'm not betting on best case.

I shake my head. I try to speak but I can't make a sound. It's like those very bad dreams, only this is so real I can smell the cops' sweat. My hand is shaking on the gun as if it weighs far more than it really does. I'm not sure I could drop it. It's like I can't even move.

If I don't drop the gun, the cops will perforate me with so much lead that my parents won't have anything to bury. I lift the gun above my head.

A big cop moves in closer. "We said drop it."

The cop's gun looks like a cannon. At the end of the barrel is a tube of silver. Baker would know what it's called. All I know is that it's to deaden the sound of the gunfire so the officer doesn't get disoriented.

The cop's hand reveals a tiny tremor.

Big gun. Jumped-up cop. Not good.

I try again to speak. "It's not me."

The cop looks at me like I've spoken a strange language.

"Not me."

Another cop swings in behind me, and I see him grab Zoe and push her to the floor. More cops join him. I shift so that my back is to the wall. Josh is on the floor in front of me. We're ringed by cops.

I see myself on a playground swing and maybe my life does flash before my eyes. If so, it doesn't take long. I hear Zoe cry out, "He's not the shooter."

More cops storm through the doors from the caf kitchen. Maybe they don't hear her. Every gun is trained on my head.

Mr. Connor edges toward me. "Adam, give me the gun."

I look down at Josh. He's watching Mr. Connor. I feel his body tense.

Mr. Connor says, "We know you're not the shooter."

"Do they know?" I gesture with my head at all the cops. "They don't appear to know."

Mr. Connor raises his hands as if to calm the cops. He says, "He's not the shooter."

Some of the cops lower their guns a notch.

Mr. Connor steps closer. "It's over, Adam. You're safe now."

I want to believe him.

I bring the gun down from above my head. All the cops' guns come back up. I freeze.

"Adam." Mr. Connor reaches out his hand.

Two things happen at the same time. I hand the gun to Mr. Connor, and Josh lunges for it. More than two things, actually. Far more than two things, because as soon as Josh grabs for the gun, the officers open fire.

Chapter Sixteen

The noise of gunfire in the hallway is incredible. My forehead flattens in the shock wave. It is that fast. Then it stops. My eardrums feel like they are being yanked out of my head, and the hallway starts to spin. I fall to my knees and throw up.

"Paramedic!" one of the cops shouts into his radio.

I blink, trying to clear my vision. Where's Zoe? I struggle to focus. In front of me, the hallway swims with blue armored cops. "Zoe?"

A cop puts his hand on my shoulder. "She's okay."

I see her then. She's standing with her hands over her face.

"Zoe!" I call to her, and she looks at me. Tears are streaming down her face. She tries to come to me, but a cop puts his hand on her arm.

I try to get up but my feet slide. I look down. There's blood on the floor. I scramble to get up, my hands and legs covered in the blood. I touch my chest, my arms, my legs. I'm not shot. It's not my blood.

A cop pulls me out of the way.

Josh is face down on the floor. A cop kneels beside him and puts his hand on Josh's neck. The cop shakes his head.

The metal doors from the kitchen bang open and a team of paramedics blast in, pushing a gurney.

I look down at Josh. Beside him on the floor, his glasses are twisted, the lenses broken. I reach down and pick up the glasses. I straighten the metal frames the best I can. One of the lenses pops out. I hold it between my thumb and finger. I clean it on the bottom of my shirt.

The paramedics are running and I think it's weird they're in such a hurry because Josh is obviously dead. Then I see Mr. Connor.

He is on the floor. His face is contorted with pain. A cop kneels beside him, his hands pressing against Mr. Connor's thigh. Blood squirts from under the cop's hand. Josh's gun is still in Mr. Connor's hand. Another cop takes it from him and sets it on the floor.

The paramedics drop the gurney down beside Mr. Connor and surround him. They work fast. One of them holds a mask to Mr. Connor's face. Another rips bandages out of sterile packages. Finally, the cop who was applying pressure to the gunshot wound sits back on his heels. His hands are covered in blood. His face is sheet white.

Collateral damage. I bet this part of his job never feels normal.

The paramedics hoist Mr. Connor onto the gurney.

On the floor, where Mr. Connor was hiding, something catches my eye. I step to the spot and bend down. It's a photograph, a wallet-size photo, the same as the one on his desk, of his wife and baby. I pick up the photo. In it, Mrs. Connor is smiling and the baby is asleep in her arms.

I think about how Mr. Connor was sitting with his head down. Maybe he had the photo in his lap. Maybe, as he counted the moments of the lockdown, he kept his eyes on the photo. Maybe he wondered if he would see his family again.

The paramedics have the gurney up on its wheels. Mr. Connor is strapped on the gurney. He's covered with a blanket. One of his hands is out of the blanket while a paramedic adjusts an IV.

I cross to the gurney. A paramedic tells me to get out of the way. I ignore him. I place the photo in Mr. Connor's hand. Mr. Connor looks at me. His hand closes over the photo. Then, at a run, the paramedics push the gurney down the hall.

I find Zoe crouched on the floor. Someone has draped a blanket over her shoulders. I sit on the floor beside her and put my arm around her. She leans her head on my shoulder.

A cop kneels down beside us. He wants to ask us questions but I can't talk right now. He says that it's okay, to take all the time I need. But I'm not sure there's going to be enough time, ever.

All kinds of cops surround Josh's body, snapping cameras, taking measurements. Someone bags the revolver.

I wish they'd cover Josh.

Two regular uniform cops stand together. I hear one say, "Eleven hundred people in this school, and only the principal gets hit. How lucky is that?"

I look at Josh's body. Eleven hundred minus one. Trust Josh. He never intended to kill anyone.

Chapter Seventeen

The seawall is quiet at midmorning, just a few cyclists and runners on the path. "Okay, Adam, last interval. Running for one minute." Mr. Connor snaps a stopwatch in his right hand. Beside him, I break into a run. One minute, and I feel every single second. Finally, the stopwatch beeps and I drop into a walk.

One minute running, nine minutes walking. We do that six times. Next week we'll work up to two minutes running, eight minutes walking. Slow steps, Mr. Connor says. He says that he learned to run this way the first time, that it will work for both of us now. In a couple of months, we'll be running ten and walking one, the same pattern that marathoners use.

Mr. Connor has been out of a cast for a few weeks but his leg still looks white. It's smaller than the other leg—wasted from being in the cast. I take a swig from my water bottle. Mr. Connor could still outrun me. He could have outrun me even in the cast. But I like this kind of running. I like the way the air smells like the sea. And it beats Mr. Ellington's gym class.

That's the deal. I run with Mr. Connor and I don't have to attend gym.

It's a good deal.

Mr. Connor and I walk back to the school. I say, "It looks almost normal, doesn't it?"

For days after the lockdown, media trucks crowded the school. News reporters clung to every doorway, looking for students with a story. Natalie got a lot of press, of course. She enjoyed it. She told everyone how Zoe and I tried to stop Josh. It's weird, though. Some people think I was in on the shooting. They want to know how I knew where Josh would be. They think that's why Josh didn't shoot us in the washroom. That Josh and I were friends. That I knew about the shooting. They even say that I was the one with the gun. That I set up Josh. That I got him killed.

Not a lot of people think that. Just some people.

People look for an answer.

After the lockdown, some of the students wanted to lower the flag to half-mast because of Josh, but parents wouldn't allow it. Baker lowered the flag anyway, and I'm glad he did.

For weeks after the lockdown, you couldn't move in front of the school for parents' vehicles dropping off and picking up kids, as if dropping off and picking up could prevent the worst from happening within the school. Now people are walking to school again. Now the parents who still drop off and pick up don't have quite the same crazed wariness on their faces.

When you come so close to losing someone, things will never again be exactly the same. For a while, my parents got weird. They made all my favorite things to eat and let me leave dirty laundry on the floor, and my little sister took out the trash for me. Now we're back to lentil casserole, but that's okay. I hug my little sister before I leave for school.

Now the front of the school looks like it does every day before lunch. A few students lounge on the front steps. Behind the windows, people move about in the classrooms.

Almost normal. Normal to the extreme. I can't think about this school anymore without thinking about Josh.

Mr. Connor turns to me. He says, "They didn't even have a funeral."

He's thinking about Josh too.

Mr. Connor continues, "They said they didn't want to draw any more negative attention to their son." He pauses. "What must it be like for them, waking up every day without him?"

I say, "The day it happened, just before

lunch, you got a call on your cell phone. Did you always know the shooter was Josh?"

He nods. "Josh's mother found a letter. She called the school."

I look at him. "Like a suicide letter?"

Mr. Connor says, "More like a will. It sounded like he was taking care of things."

Like the note he left with the hamster cage. Josh's mom gave it to me when I went to get the hamster. It's Josh's hamster now. I just take care of it. I never bring it to school. I say, "Trust Josh."

Mr. Connor claps me on the shoulder. "You'll be with us for the rest of the day?"

I smile. "I'm meeting Zoe for lunch. She'll make me attend classes this afternoon."

"Trust Zoe," he says.

I do. I don't want to turn back time, not now. I want to keep moving ahead. I'm starting to trust myself.

From a second-floor classroom, a student pauses at the window and looks down. She waves at Mr. Connor and he waves back. Then her gaze falls on me and she quickly looks away. Almost normal.

Mr. Connor says to me, "If you're off my radar, I guess I can go hunt down Baker."

"Oh, good luck with that."

Mr. Connor laughs. Then his face gets serious. He says, "Adam, thank you."

"For the run, right?"

He smiles. "Yeah. Thanks for the run."

Mr. Connor starts up the steps to the school. I pause to stretch my aching calf muscles. No pain, no gain. I follow Mr. Connor up the steps.

Chapter Eighteen

Instructions for Hamster
(Her name is Amergin)

Food: She likes seed mix. I buy her the kind with extra sunflower seeds because she likes those. Don't fill her bowl too full or she'll kick seeds all over your room. Hamsters do that. It's normal. You can feed her some apple if you want, but she really likes sunflower seeds. She also likes peanuts. Make sure they are the kind with no salt.

Water: Change her bottle often. It gets gross if you don't change it.

Cage: Use cedar shavings. They smell nice. Try to change the shavings before they get smelly. When I clean the cage, I put Amergin in my shirt pocket. She likes being in my pocket. If you don't have a shirt pocket, you can put her in a big bowl or something, but make sure she can't climb out. She's a very good climber. Clean the tray part of her cage with mostly water and just a little soap you use to wash dishes. Don't use anything too strong because she has to live in it. You don't need to wash the bars of her cage unless they get gross. Ditto for her wheel.

She likes to chew on toilet-paper rolls. And she loves cotton balls to make a nest. I give her new cotton balls when I clean her cage. I put a little bit of her old nest in with the new cotton balls so that it smells like her home.

Other: She'll try to get out of her cage. That's normal. She's used to being held.

Just be gentle and don't scare her. She's been through a rough time. Maybe just let her be quiet.

Josh

Diane Tullson has written seven novels for young adult readers, including *Saving Jasey* and *Blue Highway*. *Red Sea* (Orca), a contemporary, true-to-life adventure of piracy on the Red Sea, has been named an American Library Association Best Book and a New York Public Library Book for the Teen Age, and has been nominated for the Arthur Ellis Award and the ALA Quick Picks for Reluctant Readers. In *Red Sea*, Diane Tullson draws from her own experiences sailing in Europe for eighteen months with her husband and two young sons. *Resource Links* says: "This is a book that needs to be in every library for readers grade seven and up."

Diane Tullson was born in Calgary, Alberta. She has a BA in English literature from the University of Calgary and has studied journalism and editing. Before becoming an author, Diane worked in newspaper, radio and travel. Tullson began writing non-fiction essays for *Canadian Living* and *Westworld Magazine*. Her young adult books have been shortlisted for White Pine, Red Maple and Stellar awards.

Diane Tullson is a member of the Canadian Children's Book Centre, Vancouver Children's Literature Roundtable, Children's Writers and Illustrators of British Columbia, and the Writers Union of Canada. She speaks to schools across Canada and has presented at the University of Alberta symposium "Rethinking Literacy Education: Preparing New Teachers." Diane Tullson lives with her family in Delta, British Columbia.

Orca Soundings

Orca Soundings

Visit www.orcabook.com for Orca titles.

Other Orca Soundings by Diane Tullson

The Darwin Expedition
Diane Tullson
978-1-55143-676-0 PB
978-1-55143-678-4 HC